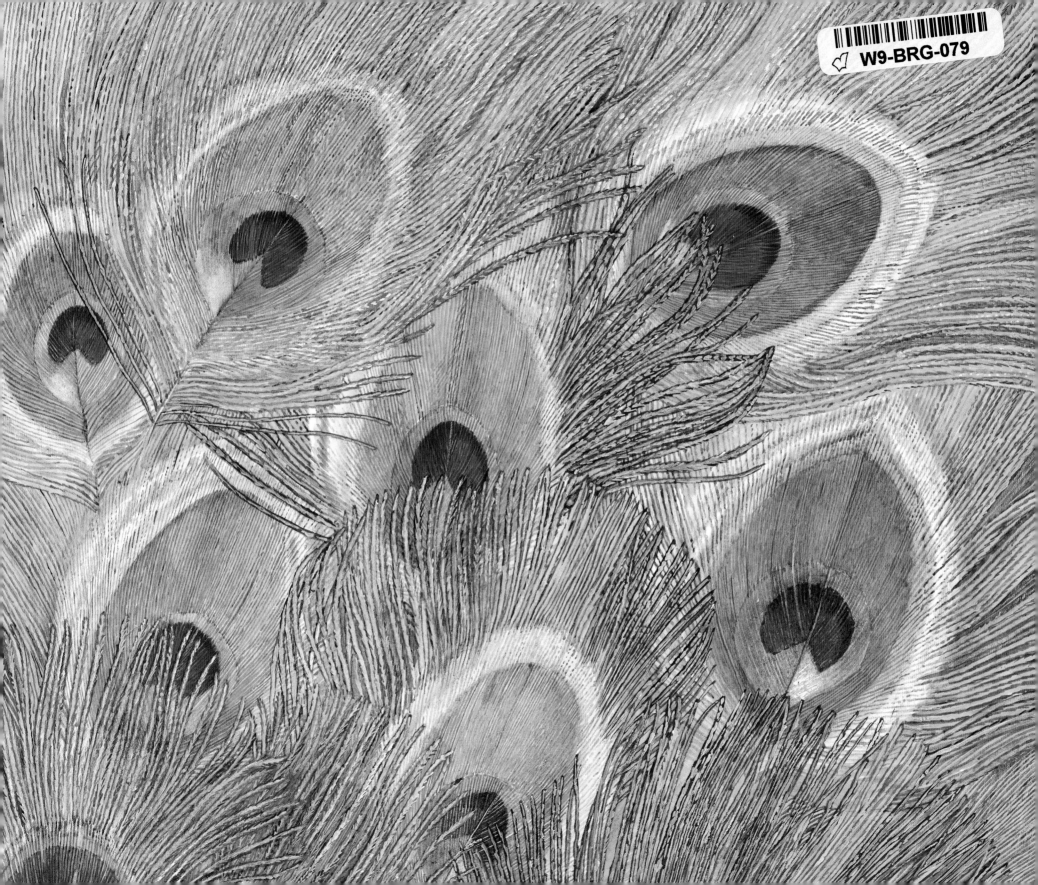

The TALE of the
TIGER SLIPPERS

JAN BRETT

putnam

G. P. PUTNAM'S SONS

For Isaac Ian Hearne

Thank you to Indrani Chatterjee,
Professor of History, University of Texas at Austin,
and Mana Kia,
Assistant Professor of Indo-Persian Studies, Columbia University,
for their insights.

G. P. PUTNAM'S SONS
an imprint of Penguin Random House LLC, New York

Visit us online at penguinrandomhouse.com

Library of Congress Cataloging-in-Publication Data is available upon request.

Manufactured in China by RR Donnelley Asia Printing Solutions Ltd.
ISBN 9780399170744
1 3 5 7 9 10 8 6 4 2

Design by Marikka Tamura. Text set in Minister Std.
The art for this book was done in watercolors and gouache.
Airbrush backgrounds by Joseph Hearne.

I live in a big house my father built
and I love to bound around the garden.

My friends are always curious
about one thing, though.
"Why is there a pair of raggedy slippers
in that fancy fountain?" they ask.

This is the story
my father tells them.

When I was a cub, I lived with my mother under the roots of a banyan tree. We were very poor, and I helped as best I could.

Mother saw how sharp thorns and stones hurt my foot pads when I worked, and she made me thick slippers. "These slippers will protect and guide you," she said. "And there is room to grow."

I was looking down at my new slippers when I saw a streak of white in the stream bank. It was silky clay that could be easily molded into shapes.

I made bricks from the clay and built my mother a pretty house.
When others saw it, they asked, "Could you build *me* a pretty
house from your bricks?"
So I did.

Years went by and the slippers seemed to guide my every step. I dug
clay, made bricks, and built houses, towers, and bridges all over the land.
Soon I had everything I could want, and I built a grand house
for my future bride.

On my wedding day, a great feast was planned. But as I went to greet my tiger bride, a crocodile poked his snout out of the stream.

"Look at those raggedy slippers," he scoffed. "What kind of elegant bridegroom are you with those old slips on your feet?"

I looked down at my dependable slippers. They were dirty and worn from hard work. But at the croc's taunts, I slipped them off and let them float away down the stream.

Faster and faster my slippers sailed in the current until they reached the village dam and stopped it up.

The waters rose, flooding the banks, until an elephant
saw the problem. He unplugged the castaway slippers and
brought them back to me.

A few months later, the tigress and I were settled in our home when word
came that the rhino king would pass by our village. He needed a place to stay,
so we readied our finest rooms.

A stork, seeing the activity, fastened his beady eyes on my slippers.

"Scandal!" he croaked. "The rhino king will be insulted by his host wearing raggedy old slippers."

I wanted to put my best foot forward for such a lofty guest, and he was about to arrive. I quickly removed my old slippers and tossed them over the wall.

When the last goat in a great herd of goats felt the *thump,*
thump of my slippers falling from the sky, she bolted.
Then all of the goats scattered, barging into houses, toppling
watermelon carts, and sinking dinghies in their panic.

The furious goatherd brought back the slippers
and demanded payment for damaged property.

In time, we celebrated the birth of our first tiger cub. Animals came from far and wide with best wishes for our new arrival. The mongoose wished him playfulness. The peacock wished for beauty, the rhino for strength, and the elephant for wisdom.

The monkey, though, added, "I wish the baby cub's father would never wear junky old slippers!"

The monkey had a good point.

I tried again and again to lose the old slippers, but they always came back.

Finally, I sent them by air to my old uncle who lived in a distant village.

When my uncle saw the frayed old slippers—worn out by hard work, and sewn
by his sister—he wept with pride. He packed a few things and set off to see us.

Uncle Ali arrived carrying a gift, and inside were the slippers.
"I know you will always want to remember how far you have come
and the good work you have done when you see these slippers,"
he said. "How they show the years!" He smiled.

The next morning I was in the garden with my son.
"I am back where I started from," I said. "What am
I going to do with these old slippers?"

My cub had the answer.

"Why not build the slippers a special house of their own? They can be seen and remembered for their place in your life, and you can wear magnificent new ones!"

So I did. From that day forward, I looked to the future, dreaming of new adventures.
And once in a while, I smile fondly at the raggedy old slippers.

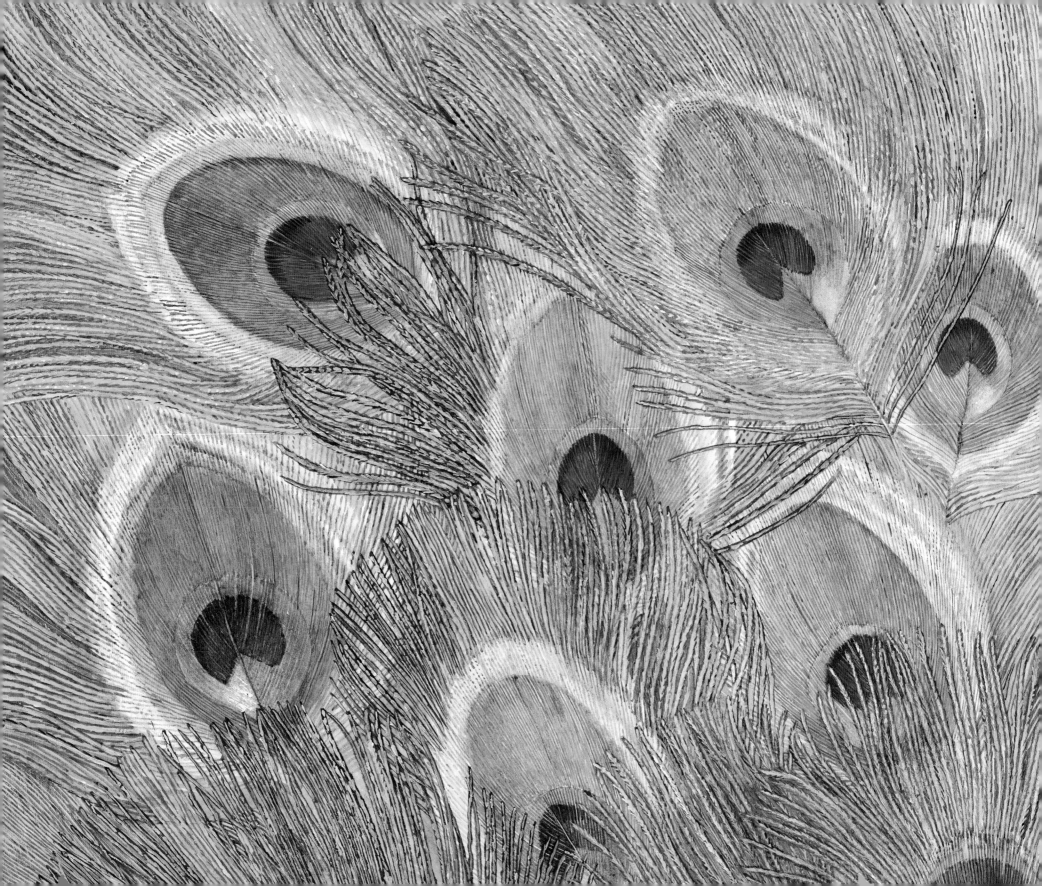